I AM YOU.

By Akash Santosh Kumar

For those who wish for more, but get only what they deserve.

Author's Note

This book was born in a place that felt both new and strange, where life moved differently than I was used to. Every line here comes from a part of me I didn't know existed. A depth I'm still discovering, still learning to face.

Within these pages, love and longing intertwine with envy and obsession, grief dances with loneliness, and moments of peace shimmer sparks a quiet enlightenment.

These words are close to my heart. I hope you find in them a reflection of your own heart, a long-forgotten spark, a whisper of hope, a shadow of love, or the ache of heartbreak. Let them meet you where you are.

Thank you for pausing here, for stepping into these fragments of my heart, and carrying them with you, even for a moment.

Contents

Alone..5

Rain.. 6

Pebble stone.. 7

When i ask.. 8

You..9

i.. 10

Deserving...11

Oh God..12

i wish...13

Hidden Truth..14

Envy...15

Breath..16

Moonlight Sunlight... 17

That night.. 18

Final morning...19

when i die.. 20

Alone

Alone, why do I feel alone?
I live with my family
three meals a day, fresh
clothes, roof over my head.

Alone, why do I feel alone?
Four walls surround me, hearing
the echoes of my heartbeat,
The witness to all my doings.

Alone, why do I feel alone?
The book on the shelf waiting
to be read, the book on the table
waiting to be written.

Alone, why do I feel alone?
I have a mind to think,
a body to move, a heart
to live.

Alone, why do I feel alone?

Rain

My ears rumble as water taps the window.
My eyes open as a response.
The wind breaks the peace of our connection.
It is rather strange really, how I am unable to move.

I lie there, staring at the rotating fan above.
Is that what broke my peace?
The window bursts open,
clothes fly over my face.

I can no longer see.
My peace, my . . . my connection.
It's gone.

Pebble stone

I kicked a pebble stone. No origin, no use.
I kicked a pebble stone, into the vast mist
we call, night.
I kicked a pebble stone, breaking the flow
of nature.
I kicked a pebble stone, the sound echoes
with the howl of the wind.
I kicked a pebble stone.
She kicked a pebble stone.

When i ask

When i ask you how your day was,
i really mean, i want to know
how each step on the concrete felt,
how each touch of the leaf felt,
how each bite of the food felt.
Mostly,
how each thought of me felt.

You

You.
Every breath breathes you.
Every sight sees you.
Every touch touches you.
Every taste tastes you.
For I am you.

i

i
How can i fall in love?
How can i connect with your soul?
How can i crave your love?
How can i hear your pumping chest?
How can i hear your shallow breath?

How can i long for your gaze?
How can i exist near you?
How can i call myself human?
When all i want is you.

Deserving

Do I deserve this?
Am I allowed? Is this a sin?
Am I allowed? Why me?
Am I allowed?

My skin yearns to lay eyes again.
Am I allowed?

My fingers, lips, eyes twitch at every
thought of her.
Am I allowed?

I no longer control my own feelings.
This is it.

Do I deserve this?

Oh God

Oh God, Oh, God, I need her.
I want her. Oh God, I want
her every breath to be mine.

Oh God, I am a sinner. Oh God,
I want everything she touches,
to be mine.

Oh God, I am stuck.
Oh God, I want those lips.
Oh God, I want those hips.
Oh God, I want those eyes.
Oh God... oh god.

i wish

i wish. i wish. i wish.
i wish time stood still.
i wish i could make love everyday.
i wish i could wake up another day.
i wish her thoughts are filled with my face.
i wish... i had more time.
i wish. i wish. i wish.

Hidden Truth

How could I have told her?
How could *I* have told her?
When I didn't even tell myself.
My life thus far has been
like a drop of rain on a window,
whatever happens, nothing ends well.

How could I have told her?
How could *I* have told her?
She was my force, my sole purpose.
Her every heartbeat,
that is all I need.

How could I have told her?
How could *I* have told her?
Time never waits. Nobody does.
I follow her dark bold round eyes,
down to her blood red lips,
down her breathing chest.

How could *I* have told her?
My breath was in its final days.

Envy

I am envious of everything that
submits to your touch. I envy
the water you drink, the food you eat,
the things that attract your gaze,
the clothes on your figure,
the hair on your head,
the nails on your fingers.

I envy each second that goes by
where I am not in your thoughts.
I envy all that set eyes on you,
the scent of your soul.

I envy your soul,
for it has more hidden within
than I can obtain, inside
this lifetime or next.

Breath

Every breath I drew, marked
a new memory of her.
Every breath I drew, the more
I felt myself drifting away,
out at sea amongst the sharks,
the fish, perhaps, that was all I was.

Every breath I drew gave
birth to wish for a little
more time. Only if,
only if, i could walk for
longer than twenty
minutes.

Every breath I drew, I knew.
I knew it's coming.

Moonlight Sunlight

The night cast a bright white
light across her face.
The bridge we stood glowed under
the moonlight. The texture of
the wind, sliced through her hair,
reflecting sunlight.

Her eyes look far into the abyss,
almost longing for something
dear. Her nose twitch as each
cool air runs across it.

Her lips, blood red, stare at me
brightly. I could only wish for
our lips to connect on that
bridge.

Her existence blinds my eyes yet
I don't look away,
rather I can't.

That night

That night, hand against hand,
lips against lips, breath against breath.
We expressed the floating feeling.

That night, snow melodramatically
flew through the miniscule crack
onto her naked stomach.

That night, gently, yet passionately, I caress her,
sliding down her body.

That night, was dark,
but our intimacy was bright.

That night, we lay,
body against body,
exchanging all we each had to offer.

That night, love had won.

Final morning

We sat there, deep in sorrow,
while I was deep in my burrow.

Her sun kissed face,
her sun kissed lips.

Her dark brown eyes
wandered into my soul,
finding a solution.

I embraced her.

We sat there, deep in sorrow.

when i die

when i die, whether below or above,
they'll only find you,
for i am only you.

when i die, whether below or above,
they'll only remember you,
for i am only you.

The thought, the smell, the sight,
the emotion, the love, the hatred,
the lust, the fear,
it'll only remind them of you.

For *i am* only *you.*

About the Author

Akash Santosh Kumar is a young, award-winning filmmaker and writer who captures the raw realism of human nature. His work delves into the hidden and often overlooked depths of emotion and thought, creating experiences that feel deeply personal and unforgettable. *I Am You* is his intimate poetic exploration of love, obsession, and the surrender of self in the presence of the beloved.